THE LOVE THAT STAYED

A STORY OF FORBIDDEN LONGING

ANUPREET

Made with ❤ on the Notion Press Platform
www.notionpress.com

For a love that never dies—
even when everything else did.
And for anyone who has ever loved quietly,
bravely, and without permission.
This story is yours.

Contents

Preface   *vii*

Acknowledgements   *ix*

About the Author   *xi*

1. Beginnings   1

2. A Woven Bond   6

3. Crossing The Line   21

4. Love's Limits   33

5. Aftermath   39

Preface

This is more than a love story.

It's a story about connections—about finding love, losing it, and learning to live with the ache of memories. It's about the moments that define us, the people who shape us, and the love that never leaves us, even when life takes us in different directions.

A tale of love, pain, and longing—written with ink, and also with the fragments of a heart that once belonged to someone else

Acknowledgements

This Book is more than simply words— it is a journey of love, heartbreak, imagination, and healing.

I want to express my heartfelt gratitude to Nima–My friend, my guide, and like a mother to me. Your unwavering trust has always been my strength. Mrugaja – For inspiring me to turn my thoughts and emotions into poems and stories. Your belief in my creative voice brought this book to life.

To every reader – Thank you for holding space for this story. To sense its silences, breathe its pauses, and carry its heart with your own. Some stories stay with us long after they end—this is one of them.

About The Author

Anupreet is a corporate HR professional, counsellor, poet, and painter—an observer of people, emotions, and the quiet stories they carry.

The Love That Stayed is her debut work of fiction, inspired by real conversations, lived silences, and one story that left a permanent mark on her soul.

Her poetry and paintings often explore themes of healing, longing, and emotional truth. She believes that some narratives don't stem purely from imagination, but from deeply personal and shared human experiences.

Through her writing, Anupreet hopes to give voice to the love stories that often remain unspoken.

You can follow Anupreet on Instagram @authoranupreet2025 or reach out via email at anupreetofficial2025@gmail.com to connect, collaborate, or simply share a story that moved you.

ONE
BEGINNINGS

The office had its usual air of quiet intensity—the soft murmuring of employees, the rhythmic clicking of keyboards, and the occasional ringing of a phone. The aroma of brewed coffee mingled with the chill of the air-conditioned office.

I walked in, dressed as always in my casual hoodie and jeans—a silent rebellion against the professional stiffness of corporate life.

As the General Manager of this IT firm, I handled operations, staff coordination, and most importantly—the company's accounts and financial oversight. I exceeded a mere system part—I oversaw its functionality.

My job demanded precision, problem-solving, and decision-making. But I preferred to keep things simple. No airs, no authority games—only the work. I wasn't here to impress anyone with formal attire.

I subsequently saw her.

She sat in the lobby, unaware of the hushed impact she had on the surrounding space. Simple black top and jeans clung to her body, the dark fabric stressing the warmth of her whitish complexion. Loose strands of her hair fell around her face, slipping free from a small clip, and, she tucked them back.

For a fleeting moment, surprise seized me. Something about her presence unsettled me—not negatively, but in a way I didn't fully understand.
I shook it off and headed straight to my cabin. Another applicant, I assumed. Another day, another routine.
I had settled into my seat when my desk phone rang.
"Ma'am, the candidate for the HR interview is here," the receptionist informed me.
I stiffened. Interview?

The door creaked open, and she stepped inside.
"Good morning, madam."
Rama looked up from her desk, offering a welcoming smile.
I didn't bother. My eyes remained fixed on my
screen, fingers tapping away at the keyboard as if I hadn't heard a thing.
She had come to meet Rama, after all. It's not me.
Her reason for being here was clear. My MD, in his infinite wisdom, had decided to bring in a new accountant—without consulting me. The same accounts I had been managing, the same work I had been handling effectively she appeared. Across from us, they didn't notice my quiet anger.
Rama, ever the professional, began the conversation. "So, Mr. Khanna reached out to you?"
"Yes, ma'am," she replied. "He asked me to meet you regarding the accountant's position."
I clenched my jaw and kept typing, my irritation simmering

beneath the surface. I created this department. If someone joined my accounts team, at the very least, they should have informed me.

I finally stole a glance at her—a quick flick of my eyes.

She sat upright, hands resting on her lap, her expression composed yet curious. It's possible she sensed the cold air I sent her way. It's possible she refrained from doing so. In either case, I wouldn't simplify this.

So, I returned to my job, ignoring her presence.

Let Rama handle it. I had nothing to do with this.

Or so it seemed.

The day had dragged on longer than usual. I buried myself in my work, pretending the morning's interview hadn't happened.

By evening, the office had settled into its usual quiet hum. Most employees had left; the HR desk held almost no one, and I finally leaned back, rubbing my temples.

That's when Rama casually dropped the bomb.

"She's joining," she said, stuffing some files into her bag.

I froze. "What?"

"She'll be handling accounts now," she continued as if she hadn't a moment before turned my entire day upside down. "So, you'll need to hand things over to her."

I stared at her, waiting for her to say. "She wasn't jokong. That wasn't the case."

Anger bubbled inside me.

After all this time spent managing the numbers, resolving financial problems, and ensuring a smooth operation—so unexpectedly, I needed to relinquish my duties? And for what? Because my boss suddenly concluded I fell short?

I clenched my jaw. "Did he even consider informing me?"

Rama sighed. "You are aware of his personality. Don't take

it personally."
But how was it possible for me to avoid it? It seemed like a betrayal. Like my efforts had been disregarded.
I grabbed my bag, my mind racing with frustration. As I walked out of the office that evening, I told myself one thing—I won't continue in this organization.
No matter what.

A Mentor's Concern

Rama leaned against my desk, arms crossed, watching me struggle with an Excel sheet that refused to balance. She had that knowing look on her face—the one that meant she had something to say but was waiting for me to acknowledge it first.
"You've been off," she said, breaking the silence.
I sighed, rubbing my temples. "It's nothing."
"It's not nothing, dear. I am familiar with you. Something's bothering you."
I hesitated before responding. "The company is planning to bring Samirah on board."
Rama didn't look surprised. She nodded, as if she had already expected this. "And that's why you've been drowning yourself in work instead of facing it."
I shrugged. "It's complicated."
She pulled a chair beside me. "Listen, I understand what Samirah's presence means to you, but you need to start speculating about yourself. "There's a world outside this office, friend. And you're letting it pass you by."
I sighed, closing my laptop. I understand. But it's not that simple."
She smiled knowingly. "It is, if you let it be."

Over coffee in the cafeteria, Rama dropped the conversation she had been holding back.

"I have something for you," she said, sliding a business card toward me.

I picked it up hesitantly. "What is this?"

"A company I've been talking to. They have an opening—one that suits you perfectly. They want someone sharp, detail-oriented, and experienced in operations. I already gave them your name."

I stared at her, surprised. "You what?"

Rama chuckled. "You need a push. You've been stuck in one place for too long, and now, with Samirah possibly joining, it'll only get harder. It's time to move forward."

I looked at the card, the company's name staring back at me. A different place, a fresh start. The idea was tempting.

"I don't know if I'm ready," I admitted.

"You're more than ready," she countered. "All you need is belief in it."

For the next few days, I pondered Rama's words. About the offer. About Samirah.

Then one evening, as I sat in my cabin staring at my resignation letter draft, I realized I had already made the decision.

Rama found me still at my desk after hours. She leaned against the doorway, arms crossed. "So?"

I turned my screen toward her, the resignation email glowing in the dim office light.

A slow smile spread across her face. "Proud of you."

I took a deep breath and hit send.

It was time to move on.

ᐯᐯᐯ

TWO
A WOVEN BOND

A decision was made. I departed.

Once my notice period commenced, I immersed myself in work, concluding outstanding tasks, ensuring no one would blame me afterward. If they wanted her to take over my role, fine—I would train her, hand over my responsibilities, and walk away without looking back.

Subsequently, she became a member.

I had convinced myself I wouldn't care, that I would stay indifferent. But the moment she stepped into the office as an employee, something seemed different.

Despite her replacing me, I harboured no anger toward her. Not completely.

That morning, Rama, Samirah, and I now shared the same workspace.

I kept things professional—no unnecessary warmth, but no visible coldness either. Her presence here was undeniable, despite my feelings.

"Sit with us for the next few days," I told her, gesturing toward the empty chair. "Merely observe. See how things run here?"

She nodded, settling in quietly.

For the next few hours, she watched as Rama and I worked, her eyes sharp, taking in every detail. I sensed her presence, her quiet attentiveness, but I didn't let it bother me. This was short-lived.

I needed to overcome this.

Afterward, I would leave.

Despite my initial annoyance, I recognized a captivating quality in her presence.

One day, Rama took leave, and Samirah brought Pav Bhaji to the office—probably because she had once heard me mention I liked it. I initially refused since I had already eaten, but when I saw the disappointment on her face, I gave in.

I took a bite. It proved unbelievable.

I glanced at her. "You got this from somewhere, or…?"

She grinned. "Homemade."

"That caught me off guard, "You cook?"

She shrugged. "I try."

I cracked a smirk. "If this is you 'try,' I wouldn't mind being a part of your experiment every day."

Her genuine, carefree laugh somehow brightened the office atmosphere.

That day, something shifted.

We started exchanging small thoughts, talking about work, random things, even personal quirks.

The next day, she casually placed a small piece of chocolate on my desk in the morning. "You like sweets, right?"

I raised a brow but accepted it. It became a habit.

Some days, she'd bring something from her tiffin and nudge it toward me with a casual, "Taste this."

Other days, I'd share my coffee and say, "Try this, way better than yours."

Before I realized it, these insignificant moments had become something more significant.

We started cracking jokes, teasing each other over accounting mistakes, creating our own small world in that office.

Proximity to her seemed simple and natural.

And I didn't understand it at the time, but that was the day our friendship truly began.

Eventually, Samirah started working from a distinct branch—the one where I worked.

Initially, I dismissed it. It may have been simpler for her to learn from me. It might have been something else.

One afternoon, I walked into the branch and saw her at her desk, typing away. Every muscle in her body was rigid, a statue of anxiety.

Something was not right.

I leaned against the doorframe, arms crossed. "You okay?"

She looked up. For a second, I saw hesitation flicker in her eyes. Afterward, she produced a weak smile and shook her head.

"Yeah... I'm fine."

She did not.

I perceived it in her clasped hands, in her avoidance of my gaze.

"If there's anything you want to talk about, you can," I said, my voice softer than before. No pressure, only an open door.

For a moment, she stayed still. afterward, without warning, she stood, came to me... and hugged me.

Tightly.

It was more than a hug.

It represented a breakdown. A moment when she could not maintain composure.
I experienced everything—
The rapid thumping of her heartbeat.
The way she clutched onto my hoodie, as if letting go would break her.
The warmth of her arms wrapping around me, melting into me.
The way she buried her face in my shoulder.
Freshly washed, silky strands of her hair brushed against my skin. A soft scent lingered—Nike Extreme.
Subsequently—her lips accidentally brushed my shoulder.
It meant nothing.

And yet, it represented something.
Something that shouldn't have mattered.
But it did.
I had hugged plenty of people in my life. Comforted colleagues, consoled friends, supported those in pain.
But this—this differed.
And I did not know why.

Samirah sat across from me, her fingers twisting together, restless. The self-assurance she possessed disappeared, replaced by something I observed in her—uncertainty.
Her eyes flickered toward me, hesitant. Finally, she spoke.

"He called me."
I frowned. "Who?"
She swallowed hard. "Him."
I didn't need her to explain. I was already aware. The man who had left her heart in pieces—the one who never truly left her mind.

"After a year..." her voice barely exceeded a whisper. "He wants to come back."

A strange silence settled between us.

I studied her carefully. Conflict filled her eyes, a war between her past and her future.

I leaned back, keeping my tone neutral. "And what do you want?"

She exhaled sharply, shaking her head. I lack awareness.

Subsequently, in a voice barely audible, she admitted, "I loved him, but he's still married. He's not ready to leave his wife. I'm unsure whether I should meet him or proceed.

My fingers tapped against the table, my mind racing.

"I have no issue with seeing him," I said evenly. "But getting back into a relationship with a married man? That's a problem, Samirah. Do you really want to be in a place where you'll always come second?"

She lowered her gaze, gripping her wrist as if the motion would ground her.

"He says he loves me," she murmured. "That he needs me."

I sighed, leaning forward. "Samirah, men like him... they never choose. They keep both worlds intact because neither one is inconvenient enough to leave. And the woman they love? She's the one for whom they don't expect to wait.

Her fingers stilled. She heard now.

Should you encounter him, conclude the matter.

She looked up at me, her eyes searching mine, as if hoping I'd give her permission to hold on. But I wouldn't.

Before some truths set you free, they must hurt.

After a long moment, she exhaled. And this time, when she nodded, I understood—she actually listened.

From that day forward, things are not same in between us.

Samirah was lighter and freer, as if a weight had been removed from her shoulders. She laughed more, spoke more, and let herself be herself around me.

We started having lunch together more often. Initially, it involved only professional communication—deadlines, reports, office politics. But gradually, our conversations became personal.

Sometimes, we talked about food—

"You should try Gujarati food, Dhoklu!" she'd insist. "Dhokla is life!"

I'd roll my eyes. "Only if you promise to eat proper spicy street food with me first."

Other times, it involved music—

"Old songs have a soul," I told her one day.

She smirked. "And here I assumed you liked fast beats and rap!"

Subsequently, after work, I commenced driving her home.

It hadn't been planned. It has recently taken place.

At first, it was a simple gesture—making sure she got home safely. But over time, it became our routine.

Those quiet rides, the city lights passing by, the comfortable silence between us, became something I looked forward to.

It was during those rides that I realized—friendship is about more than words. Sometimes, it's about presence. It's about knowing someone's presence, even without words.

But not everyone welcomed this change.

Her mother, however, wasn't pleased.

It might have been my background. It may have been the fact that I wasn't from her caste. Whatever the reason, she didn't like me.

She never specified it, but I perceived it in her eyes each time I took Samirah home. The way she hesitated before acknowledging me. The way her smile never quite reached her eyes.

But Samirah... she didn't seem to care.

If anything, she started liking me even more.

She defended me, stood by me, and ensured I understood—our bond was enduring.

And perhaps I was beginning to sense the same.

Samirah's parents left town, attending a family function in another city. She and her brother were the only ones at home.

That's when she called.

"Let's go out," she said, excitement buzzing in her voice.

I hesitated for a second. It had been a long day, and I doubted my readiness to celebrate.

However, she added, "Come on, it's only one night. We'll have fun."

Somehow, she convinced her brother, and within minutes, we had a plan—The Eclipse Lounge, a rooftop cafe with a dance floor, dim neon lights, and music that made you forget reality.

That evening, when I pulled up outside her house, she stepped out of the gate... and for a moment, I forgot to breathe.

She donned a black-and-white striped t-shirt, black tights that hugged her body perfectly, and heels that made her look effortlessly elegant. The soft glow of the streetlight highlighted the delicate curve of her jaw, the warmth in her skin.

For the first time, I saw her differently.

Not as a colleague.

Not as a friend.

Only... her.

We arrived at the city lounge as the dance floor opened. Music filled the air, dim lights flickering over the wooden interiors. The city skyline stretched beyond the rooftop, a sea of twinkling lights below us.
Samirah picked up the menu, her lips curling into a mischievous smile.
"I want sex on the Beach," she said, locking eyes with me.
I nearly choked.
Her laughter rang through the air. She found this enjoyable. I found a strange satisfaction in my discomfort, the way my face heated as I awkwardly turned to the server and somehow managed to order the drink without fumbling over the words.

I saw the satisfaction on her face. She loved getting a reaction out of me.
Two drinks in, and she buzzed—playful, carefree, her laughter echoing over the music.
Without a word, she took my hand and pulled me toward the dance floor.
Her body swayed to the rhythm, eyes closed, lost in the moment.
I should have danced with her.
But I could not.
I remained there, watching her—completely mesmerized.
Something inside me shifted. Something I hadn't known before.
My feelings for her exceeded simple care.
I loved spending time with her.
I empathized with her.
And suddenly, she no longer remained merely my colleague

or my friend.

She is Samirah.

And in that moment, she became my responsibility in ways I hadn't realized before.

We danced, laughed, and ate; for the first time in a long time, I didn't dwell on work, my future, or my problems.

I had been there—in her company.

And perhaps I wished that night would last forever.

By the time we got back to her house, the night had settled into a comfortable silence.

The laughter, the teasing, the music—it all faded into a stillness that neither of us wanted to break.

She unlocked the door, stepping inside first, and afterwards turned to look at me.

"Stay," she whispered. Until morning.

Her voice showed no hesitation. Sheer quiet certainty.

Fatigue overcame her. And for once, I didn't argue.

A moment of distinct sensation.

We proceeded to her bedroom, freshened up, and lay on the bed—the space between us filled with unspoken words.

She remained there, inches away, her breathing steady, her eyes fluttering closed for a moment before opening again.

I wanted to hold her.

I wanted to kiss her.

I wanted to wrap her in my arms and never let go.

But I hesitated.

Because something had shifted between us. Something too delicate, too fragile, too real.

And I doubted my readiness to cross that unseen boundary.

The silence stretched, thick with tension.

Afterward, as if she sensed my hesitation, she whispered in

the quiet darkness,
"It's okay. Hold me."
I still didn't move.
It was impossible for me.
Because if I had, I wasn't sure, I could relinquish my hold.
Afterward, she reached for me.

Slowly, gently, she pulled me into her arms, resting her head against my chest.
And that way, we fell asleep.
But I didn't sleep right away.
I lay there, sensing the warmth of her breath against my skin, the way she fit so perfectly in my arms.
And for the first time, I realized something.
My affection for her surpassed simple appreciation.
I started to fall for her.

Perhaps excessively.
The Morning of Unspoken Truths
The next morning, before she even woke up, I left.
Not because I wanted to.

But because if I remained, my feelings were liable to reveal something I hadn't planned to confess.
After that night, we were more than colleagues. Our friendship had developed past a simple camaraderie.
We started meeting more often—coffee dates that stretched into long conversations, lunch breaks that seemed too short. There was an unspoken comfort between us, something neither of us defined but both of us sensed.

It lingered in the spaces between words, in the quiet moments where nothing needed to be said.

The ultimate day of the office arrived. I cleared my desk, pretending it was another ordinary day. If I disregarded it, perhaps it wouldn't appear tangible.

Then Samirah walked in.

She was quiet at first, standing and watching me, with an unexpressed idea in her eyes.

Slowly, she placed a small box ',in front of me.

"This is for you."

I frowned, opening it carefully. Inside lay a locket—gold, delicate, and clearly something precious.

I looked up at her in surprise. "Samirah, I can't take this. It's gold—"

"It's not about that," she interrupted, her voice softer, almost hesitant. "It's my favorite. It's been with me for years."

I exhaled, understanding the weight of this gift.

"I... want you to have it," she admitted, a flicker of vulnerability in her eyes.

For the first time in all the years I had known her, she looked afraid—not of losing something materialistic, but of losing me.

I swallowed hard.

"I can't take it. Not now."

Her face fell, and for a moment, I regretted my words. Before she could turn away, I gently placed my hand over hers.

"But I promise, I'll take it once you pass your CA final."

She blinked, processing my words. A small, understanding smile slowly appeared.

"You always push me towards my goals," she murmured.

I met her gaze. "Because you should be something in life, Samirah. And you will be."

The moment settled between us, quiet but powerful.

A gift.

A promise.

A connection that neither of us understood, yet neither of us rejected.

After I left the organization and started my new role, things changed—but not completely.

We still spoke often—sometimes on calls, sometimes over text.

Previously, there was no WhatsApp—only Google Chat, where our messages filled the screen with long conversations, teasing remarks, and silent pauses that somehow still meant something.

Despite the physical distance, our bond remained strong.

If anything, it only grew.

It was the day of her CA exam. She was supposed to leave by 2 PM.

At 12 PM, my phone rang.

Her name flashed on the screen. My chest tightened.

"Are you free?" Samirah's voice was quiet, uncertain.

Office work overwhelmed me, but something in her tone made me pause.

"What happened?"

A brief silence. Then — "Can you meet me?"

That was all she said.

Without hesitation, I finished what I could and left to see her.

We met at a cafe.

The rich, bitter aroma of freshly brewed coffee filled the air, blending with the soft hum of conversations. The cafe was neither too crowded nor too empty—a balance of quiet meetings and casual catch-ups.
But between us, the silence weighed more than the air.
She sat across from me, fingers fidgeting with the rim of her coffee cup. She hadn't even taken a sip.
I observed her. "Samirah, why didn't you give the exam?"
She didn't answer right away.
Outside, the world moved at its usual pace—people coming and going, the distant honking of cars, the rhythmic clinking of coffee cups against saucers.
But inside, between us, the world forgot to move.
Her eyes welled up.
"I don't know..."
Her sadness was more than simple disappointment.

She was breaking.
I leaned forward, my voice steady but firm.
"Look, Samirah, if you don't want to do CA, that's okay. But don't walk away because of fear."
She looked at me—and truly looked at me.
And at that time, it was apparent to both of us that this was more than exams.
It was about something deeper.
Something that didn't need definitions or explanations.
Something that lingered between us, much like the untouched coffee that had now turned cold.
We understood each other with minimal words exchanged.

[Samirah's Point of View]

The morning had been suffocating. The walls of my home

seemed to be pressing in on me. The weight of expectations, of maintaining an image, of being the perfect daughter, crushed me.

I had promised. Promised my newly found best friend that I would not let anything hold me back. That I would show up for myself.

But when the moment arrived, I froze.

I stared at my exam notes, knowing time was slipping away, yet unable to move. The pressure, the fear of disappointing everyone, wrapped around me like chains.

And I let it happen.

I missed the exam. The regret settled in immediately, bitter and unforgiving.

But it wasn't only the exam I'd failed today.
There was something else—something even more valuable.
A promise. A gift I had planned to give my best friend, one that now seemed pointless.
My mind held only that lovely spirit.

ᐅᐅᐅ

THREE

CROSSING THE LINE

It bloomed out of nowhere, like spring after a harsh winter. Samirah had begun visiting me at my new office. She traversed the city to meet me. We ate lunch together. It wasn't discussed, yet with every visit, every soft, knowing glance, something inside me stirred. One afternoon, she sat opposite me, watching as I worked. A change hung in the air—a charged silence.

I perceived her gaze tracking every action—observing my fingers fly across the keyboard, noticing my lip caught in thought.

I sensed it.
I ignored it.
Or at least, I tried to.
Then, suddenly—

She kissed me. A Moment That Changed Everything I froze. For the first time in my life, my mind went blank. I pulled back slightly, locking eyes with her, searching for something—an explanation, hesitation, anything. But she didn't hesitate. She was aware of exactly what she was doing.

And in that moment, so did I. Before I could process anything, before logic could return to my thoughts, we found ourselves in the server room. The window curtains slid shut. The world outside blurred, and only her—only us—remained. She looked at me, breathless, lips slightly parted. I'm unsure who acted first. Maybe it was her.

Maybe it was me.
But afterward—We kissed.
Desperately.

Her hands tangled in my hair, pulling me closer, pressing herself against me as if she had been waiting for this forever. I held her waist, noting the warmth of her skin through the thin fabric of her top. The taste of her breath mixed with mine—a mix of coffee, longing, and something dangerously intoxicating.

I didn't understand what was happening. Only one thing was clear to me—
I couldn't stop. Her nails dug into my back, my fingers traced the curve of her spine, and in that moment, everything else faded away. No rules. No questions. No boundaries.

Only her.
Only us.
And that was my first kiss.
A secret impossible to forget.

I couldn't focus the entire next day.

Her hands hovered above the keyboard, typing nothing, while her mind screamed everything.

The kiss.

The warmth of it.

The truth of it.

And the terrifying silence that followed.

It wasn't rehearsed. It wasn't even allowed.

It suddenly occurred.

Two women.

One kiss.

And a thousand unspoken questions that now hung heavy in the air.Samirah had barely looked at her since. At work, her eyes darted away, her voice reduced to necessary syllables. It was as if that moment had rewired everything—and now neither of us knew how to function around each other. But the discomfort was more than simple awkwardness. It was fear. Not of each other—but of what it meant.

Because girls didn't kiss girls. Not in their world. Not in the stories they were told growing up. This was more than new. It was forbidden. And yet, in the quiet corners of their minds, we both sensed something irreversible had changed. I sat at our usual cafe that evening, staring at the empty chair across from me. I could still see the ghost of Samirah's laughter there, the soft imprint of yesterday's closeness that now appeared a sin. I picked up my phone.

"We need to talk."

My fingers trembled, but I hit send.

A few seconds later, the screen lit up.

"Okay, Aarya,"

A single word. But it said everything.
We were both thinking it.
And experiencing it.
Drowning in the weight of it.
Beyond a kiss—
But a crack appeared in the world we were taught to live in.
The type of crack that may break us—
or set us free.

Some nights, the weight of life was unbearable. That night was one of them. I experienced exhaustion from work, family expectations, and never-ending responsibilities. But more than that, I was drained by myself—by the storm of questions swirling within me:
Who am I, really? What do I even want?
Why did I kiss her?
Was it only attraction?
Or did it involve something far deeper—something closer to love than I had ever dared to admit?
I didn't want to be around anyone.
Not because I was tired of people—but because I was terrified of what I had just discovered within myself.

So, I grabbed my stuff and checked into a hotel. I locked the world outside. That night, I read—page after page, chapter after chapter, escaping into other people's stories so I wouldn't have to face my own. I let their pain blur with mine, their hope soothes the ache in my chest. The words became a shelter—whispers of healing, echoes of heartbreak, reflections of everything I was too tired to say out loud. Eventually, sleep took over, wrapping me in much-needed silence. By morning, my phone rang.

Samirah.

I hesitated before answering, my voice distant. "I don't want to talk."

She didn't argue. She didn't ask questions.

Instead, she bunked office and came straight to me.

When she arrived, she didn't knock. She didn't demand explanations.

She sat beside me, silent and steady—her presence alone breaking the walls I had built overnight.

For the first time in hours, I exhaled.

"I'm all yours," she whispered, resting her hand on mine.

I looked at her, and truly saw her. And in that moment, I understood her intention.

We talked for hours—about my fears, my struggles, her insecurities.

No judgment. No pretense. Just us.

By afternoon, after a quiet lunch, we lay back on the bed, exhausted from all the words.

A shift was sensed in the air.

She was close. Too close.

I turned my head, finding her eyes already on me—searching, waiting, wanting.

We had lost our sense of self.

Perhaps, for the first time, we remembered what we truly were to each other.

A moment of inevitability.

I reached out, tucking a stray strand of hair behind her ear.

She didn't move. She didn't stop me.

My fingers lingered, trailing down the side of her face, feeling the warmth of her skin beneath my touch.

She inhaled sharply.

I swallowed hard. "Samirah..."

She didn't let me finish.

She pulled me closer.
Her breath fanned against my lips—soft, teasing, hesitant.
And then, she kissed me.
Slow at first. Testing. Searching.
Then, deeper.
Her hands found my waist, pulling me into her, moulding her body against mine.
My lips found their way to her bare shoulders, my hands tracing the warmth of her skin.
I kissed her—everywhere—losing myself in the way she responded, in the way she trembled under my touch. She gasped as my fingers explored her, her body arching into mine like she had been waiting for this moment forever.
And when she reciprocated, it surpassed simple passion.
It was surrender.
It was a connection deeper than anything we had ever spoken about.
An undeniable love.
After, as we lay tangled in each other's arms, I traced slow circles on her back.
She looked at me, her eyes dark with something deeper than desire.
Then—she said the words that changed everything.
"I'm in love with you. I don't want to lose you."
I sensed her heartbeat beneath my palm, steady yet fragile.
I held her closer, knowing the weight of those words.
Because deep down, I already knew.
I already belonged to her.

I stood at the balcony, the city lights blurring into the distance. I'd never known fear like this; it was unlike anything I'd experienced. Telling Rama meant acknowledging that I had truly fallen for Samirah.

My fingers hovered over the dial button. Would Rama understand? Or would she consider this another period?

As I hesitated, Samirah's name popped up on my screen. I answered, her voice softer than usual.

"I miss you," Samirah whispered.

I closed my eyes, leaning against the railing. "Me too." And in that moment, I knew—I had to tell Rama, no matter the consequences.

Days passed, and our love flourished. It was no longer hidden in stolen glances or secret meetings. It was in the way we laughed together, the way her fingers unconsciously brushed against mine during casual conversations. It was in the lingering warmth of her gaze when she believed I wasn't noticing. It was in the quiet moments where words weren't needed.

And surprisingly, her mother—who once hesitated about me—started liking me. Maybe she saw how much I cared for Samirah. Maybe she grasped I wasn't a temporary figure in her daughter's life. Whatever the reason, she no longer looked at me with doubt. Her gaze softened, her words became kinder. And for a moment, I thought things could be alright.

But Rama...

Rama was different.

Rama knew everything.

About me.

About my feelings.

About Samirah.

She had always been the one person who understood me without explanations. She was my anchor, my mentor, my family in ways blood relations never could be. Her approval meant the world to me. And for a while, I believed I had it. But then, something shifted. One evening, as we sat together, she exhaled deeply and looked at me. "Aarya... be careful." I frowned. "What do you mean?" She hesitated, as if choosing her words carefully. "Loving someone is beautiful. But loving someone who might not fight for you... that's dangerous." Her words unsettled me. I wanted to tell her that my love for Samirah was real. That it wasn't simply a phase or a reckless emotion. But when I tried, the words never seemed enough. Because deep down, I knew—if Rama didn't approve, something was truly wrong. And though I was unaware, that moment would change everything.

Life at home was becoming unbearable. The daily arguments. The suffocating expectations. The constant reminder that no matter how much I achieved, I was still only a daughter, not an individual. One day, my mother uttered the words I had been fearing. "You should get married." I knew it was coming. But the moment those words left her lips, something inside me rebelled. As an independent woman, I wasn't ready to surrender my life to someone else. More than that... I wasn't ready to leave her. I wasn't ready to leave Samirah.

Marriage was never my dream. Stability was. Peace was. A place I could call my own, where I didn't have to answer to anyone. So, I made a decision. I spoke to Rama about it, and with her support, I decided to buy a house. When I told Samirah, she was surprisingly excited. "You should do it," she said, her eyes shining. "It'll be your space, your freedom." And so, the decision was made. I found a house.

The moment I stepped inside, it was immediately suitable. It smelled of fresh paint and possibilities. Sunlight streamed in through the large windows, illuminating the empty space that was soon to be mine. But what made it even more special? It was near Samirah's house, as if the universe was quietly connecting us.

The day of my housewarming pooja was special. It was greater than possessing a home. It was about creating a place where I could finally be at peace. A place where I could exist without explanations, without restrictions. Only three people knew about this house—my mother, Rama, and Samirah. The three pillars of my life. During the ceremony, I was caught up in rituals when Samirah arrived. She held a small wrapped box in her hands, her eyes shining with something, unreadable". She placed it in my hands with a small smile.

"This is for you", Aarya.
Curious, I unwrapped it. And for a moment, my breath hitched. Inside was a small silver idol, placed with care at the center of the room—its presence quiet, grounding, and full of calm. My favorite. She had remembered. I looked up at her, my throat tightening with emotion. "Samirah... this is..." She shrugged playfully, trying to act casual. "It seemed to me you ought to have Bappa in your new home." I ran my fingers over the intricate details of the idol, the cool metal warming under my touch. I said little. But I knew, at that moment, this gift held greater significance than a simple present. It was a silent promise.
A piece of her in my home, forever. Even today, that idol sits in my puja ghar. A reminder of the love that once was. A reminder of the love that always will be.

This house was more than just walls and a roof. It was our safe space. Samirah was the life of this home; she made it feel warm, lived-in, and full of laughter. She became the queen of this space, her presence filling every corner. For six to seven months, this was our world. A world that appeared so natural, so effortless—like forever. But forever is a fragile thing. Because soon, everything would change.

Mornings resembling a dream

Each morning, under the excuse of going to the gym, Samirah would come over. She would wake me up early, her voice soft yet teasing. "Lazy girl, get up," she would say, nudging me until I groaned in protest.

Then she'd walk to the kitchen, making tea like she owned the place. The scent of boiling ginger and cardamom filled the air. But I wasn't paying attention to that. I stood behind her, wrapping my arms around her waist, pressing my face into her freshly washed hair, inhaling her scent. This was my favorite part of the day. She would stiffen for a moment, subsequently relaxing into me, a small smile curving her lips.

"Aarya..." she would whisper, her voice somewhere between a protest and a plea. I would kiss the side of her neck—soft, lingering. And she would shiver. But she never pulled away. She would swat my arm playfully. "Let me make tea, at least!" I would grin, stepping back just enough to let her breath. Then we would sit on the balcony, sipping tea, watching the city wake up. And in those quiet moments, I would wonder—could this last forever?

Some days, she would bring her tiffin from home, balancing

it carefully as she walked in. She wouldn't even ask. She would sit beside me, open the box, and start serving food onto a plate. "Eat properly," she would scold, pushing a spoonful of food toward me. "You always skip meals. That's why you keep falling sick." I never argued. I let her take care of me. Because in those moments, I wasn't the independent, strong-minded woman fighting the world. I was just hers. And when she smiled in satisfaction, watching me finish my food, I knew— This was more than routine. This was love.

Every evening, without fail, we met for coffee.

It didn't matter if we were tired. It didn't matter how busy the day had been. What mattered was that we were together. Sometimes at my place, where she would make coffee exactly the way I liked it. Sometimes at a quiet cafe, where she would take tiny sips and watch me talk, as if every word I said was important. We sat close, our knees touching under the table, our hands brushing against each other when we reached for the sugar. We laughed. We teased. We shared moments that evoked the feeling of home. For six to seven months, this was our routine. A routine that appeared so natural, so effortless— As if we belonged in each other's lives forever. But forever is a fragile thing. Because soon, everything would change.

Rama had always been my guide, my silent protector. She watched over me, never interfering, but always making sure I wasn't getting lost in my emotions. One evening, as we sat on my balcony sipping tea, she looked at me, her expression unreadable. "Aarya, you need to be careful," she murmured. I sighed. "You've said that before, Rama." She didn't respond right away. She watched the sunset, as if choosing her words carefully. "She loves you. But love isn't always enough. People like Samirah... they carry the weight of family on their shoulders. Can she fight that weight for you?" I remained silent. Because deep down, I knew the answer. But I didn't want to face it yet. Rama, however, had already seen the storm before it arrived.

ppp

FOUR

LOVE'S LIMITS

The cafe was unusually quiet that evening.
Samirah sat across from me, her fingers tracing the rim of her coffee cup, eyes distant. She hadn't spoken much since we sat down, and that silence... it was unsettling.
Something was on her mind.
I waited, giving her space to say whatever was weighing on her.
And then, she said it.
"Maa wants me to get married."
The words landed like a stone in my chest.
My breath hitched—but only momentarily. I nodded, keeping my expression neutral.
"And what do you want?"
She shrugged, looking away.
"I don't know...She thinks it's time."
Her voice lacked conviction, yet there was a quiet surrender in her words.
I leaned back in my chair, forcing a small smile.
Samirah, your future is important.
I meant it.
But something about the way she stared at her coffee, in a

pensive state, hinted at more.

She sighed deeply, rubbing her temples as if trying to gather courage.

"It's not just about Maa's wish, Aarya... There's more."

I stayed silent.

"Maa has been unwell for a while. She doesn't share everything, but I see it—the medications, the frequent hospital visits. She's hiding the severity of it. On top of that, our financial situation isn't great. Appa's business is barely surviving. And with society constantly whispering about how an unmarried daughter becomes a burden... it's just too much."

Her voice cracked, but she pushed through it.

"They think if I marry Vihaan, it'll bring stability. He has a good job. A calm life. Maa thinks it'll take pressure off the family."

Vihaan.

I had heard the name before. I had ignored it every time. Until now.

I steadied myself. "And what about you? What do you feel about him?"

She paused, She breathed, "I am unsure, but I know one thing I can't be selfish. This isn't just about me anymore."

As I considered this moment's significance unsurpassable, she looked at me and added—

"Maa wants you to come with me when I meet him."

I blinked, confused. "Me?"

She nodded. She has confidence in you, Aarya.

I almost laughed at the irony.

Here I was—in love with her, being asked to help her choose someone else.

She feels you'll be an excellent judge of character.

My throat tightened. She had no idea what she was asking

of me.
Or possibly she did.
Maybe this was her way of asking me to let go.
I looked at her, searching her eyes for any sign—any hesitation. But there was none.
And so, I smiled.
A smile that barely reached my eyes.
"Of course, I'll come with you."
Even though deep down, I already knew the ending to this story.

After the meeting at the cafe Samirah sat beside me, her fingers absentmindedly playing with the edge of her dupatta.
Her face held a mix of excitement and hesitation.
"I liked him," she admitted, tucking a strand of hair behind her ear. "He seems nice... but..."
I watched her carefully. "But?"
She sighed. "His parents are from Banaras. I don't know how I'll fit in there. I'm scared of married life."
I leaned forward, my voice calm, reassuring.
"Samirah, Vihaan is staying in Pune. You'll only have to visit Banaras twice a year. If he's a good guy, that's not a big deal."
She nodded, but something in her eyes told me she wasn't fully convinced.
Still, after that day, she started talking to Vihaan more often.
Our routine stayed unchanged, but I sensed the alteration.
It was subtle, like a slow-moving storm in the distance—something you sense before it completely takes over.

Like always, after work, I called Samirah for coffee.
"Vihaan is my first appointment," she said.
That was fine with me.
I trusted her.
As planned, I reached at the Mall, waiting near our usual spot.
I called her.
She cut my call.
I tried again.
Cut.
Fifteen minutes passed.
Next, twenty.
Finally, a message.
"I'm getting late. I'll meet you later."
As I was leaving, I saw her.
She was walking out of the mall with Vihaan.
Laughing.
Lost in conversation.
As if I didn't exist.
Something inside me broke.
I turned away and left.
That night, I didn't call her.
I didn't text her.
And for the first time, she didn't call me either.
I lay awake, staring at my phone screen.
The clock ticked past midnight.
No message.
No missed calls.
A few weeks ago, she would have called me at this hour, only to talk about random things, to tell me what she ate, to ask if I had slept.
Now, there was only silence.

She was still there.
Still meeting me.
Still calling sometimes.
But I perceived it.
The distance.
It was growing.
And the worst part?
She didn't even notice it.

I held it in for days.
Pretended that everything was fine.
Told myself that she was just busy, that things hadn't changed, that she would come back.
But denial only lasts so long.
She got engaged and soon got married too.
And with that, she disappeared from my life.
She moved into Vihaan's house, and just like that—there was no contact.
Days turned into weeks.
I would stare at my phone, willing it to ring. But it never did.
One night, I sat alone in my apartment, the silence deafening. The weight of everything crushed me—the memories, the loss, the love that had no place to go.
I opened my drawer, pulling out a bottle of sleeping pills.
I didn't consider.
I didn't hesitate.
I just wanted the pain to stop.
The next thing I remembered was waking up in a hospital. The bright white lights stung my eyes. Machines beeped beside me. My throat was raw, my body weak.
I heard whispers—nurses talking, the soft hum of a ventilator. And then, Rama's voice.
She was sitting beside me, her eyes red from crying.

"Aarya," she murmured, her voice shaking. "Why?"
I turned away, unable to meet her gaze.
She gripped my hand tightly. "You don't get to do this. You don't get to leave like this."
Tears slid down my face. "She's gone, Rama."
"She was never yours to lose," Rama said softly, her words cutting through my grief. "But you? You are still here. And that matters."
The days in the hospital passed in a blur. Doctors came and went, their voices distant. They called it severe depression. They prescribed medications, therapy.
But nothing they said could fill the void Samirah left behind.

Samirah never came.
Not to the hospital. Not after.
She had stepped into her new life, and I was no longer a part of it.
There were no messages. No apologies. No explanations.
Sheer silence.
And I had to learn to live with that.

☙☙☙

FIVE

AFTERMATH

Months had passed since the hospital, since I had given up hope of hearing from her again.

Then, one evening, my phone rang.

Her name flashed on the screen.

I froze. My fingers hovered over the answer button. My heart pounded.

After all this time, why now?

I answered. "Hello?"

There was silence, then a shaky breath. "Aarya... I'm pregnant."

I gripped the edge of the table, my vision blurring. "What?"

"I don't know what to do," she whispered. "Vihaan... my understanding of him was wrong."

Her voice cracked, and before she could hide it, I heard her sobs.

A painful mix of emotions surged through me—anger, sadness, the desperate urge to comfort her despite everything.

I swallowed the lump in my throat. "Tell me everything."

Samirah never called me on her engagement.

I had expected it, had waited for it. But my phone never rang.

I found out later why—when Rama finally told me the truth.

"She wanted to talk to you," Rama admitted one evening, guilt in her eyes. "After your suicide attempt... she was desperate to reach you."

I stared at her. "Then why didn't she?"

Rama exhaled deeply. "I stopped her."

A sharp pain shot through my chest. "Why?"

"Because you were fragile, Aarya," she whispered. "And if she had come back into your life, then... you wouldn't have survived losing her again."

I was fuming and ready to lash out. Wanted to scream. But deep down, I knew Rama had only tried to protect me.

But that didn't change the ache. The knowledge that she had wanted to talk to me. That she had needed me as much as I needed her.

Despite that, we had been kept apart.

The last time we met before her marriage, she hugged me. Tight. Desperate. As if she knew this was the last time she could hold me like this.

I felt her heartbeat against mine, and for a moment, it seemed she might say something. Stop this madness. Choose me.

But she whispered, "I'll always love you."

I felt my chest crack, my breath hitch.

She pulled away before I could reply, walking away from me. Toward him.

I watched her leave, knowing I had lost her forever.

Or so it appeared.

Days passed. Then weeks. Then months.
The pain didn't fade. It only settled—like an old wound that never really heals.
Every morning, I woke up expecting a message, a call, anything.
Nothing came.
I went to work, kept myself busy, smiled when needed. To the world, I was fine.
But inside, I was hollow.
I walked past coffee shops we used to visit, heard songs we once sang together, and each time, a fresh wound reopened.
I told myself I was moving on. That I was healing.
But healing isn't about forgetting.
And I could never forget her.

Months later, she called.
Her voice was distant. Cold. As if she had accepted that we were nothing more than a memory.
"Aarya, I filed for divorce."
For a moment, I couldn't breathe.
Divorce?
I had known her marriage wasn't perfect. But this?
I gripped the phone tighter. "Samirah..."
Before I could say more, her voice broke.
"As you cursed me, see what happened. My life is scattered... I don't deserve love."
A suffocating ache gripped my chest.
I had said it once. In anger. In heartbreak.
I had cursed her. Told her she would never find love like mine.
And now... she accepted it as true.
It was her belief I caused her life's downfall.
That day, something inside me shattered.

I wanted to tell her I was sorry. That I never meant for this
to happen. That I never wanted this for her.
But it was too late.
She had already made up her mind.
And after that day, she was gone for good.

Life moved forward.
I kept going. Worked harder. Built a future.
To the world, I was strong. Unshakable.
But some nights, when I was alone, I still heard her voice.
I still felt the ghost of her touch.
I had moved forward.
But I had never truly moved on.
Because love never dies.
Some wounds never heal.
Perhaps, or possibly—
I never wanted them to.

🐾🐾🐾

I loved you in moments
no one ever saw—
in the pauses between words,
in the space between yes and no.

I loved you silently,
like rain that never reached the ground—
felt,
but never held.

You were never mine to keep,
but I carried you like breath—
natural, constant, invisible.

And though you walked away,
your footprints
still echo through me.

Some love doesn't leave.
It just stays.

By Anupreet